T0304499

Black Sun Lit
c/o Jared D. Fagen
PO Box 307
Arkville, NY 12406

www.blacksunlit.com | @BlackSunLit

Printed in the United States of America by Bookmobile
www.bookmobile.com

Distributed by Small Press Distribution
www.spdbooks.org

Black Sun Lit publications and programs are made possible by the New York State Council on the Arts with the support of the Office of the Governor and the New York State Legislature.

NO MATERIAL

Losarc Raal

BLACK SUN LIT

BROOKLYN / ARKVILLE, NY
2023

For Listeners

What makes you exist is not the force of your desire but the play of the world and seduction; it is the passion of playing and being played, it is the passion of illusion and appearance, it is that which comes from elsewhere.

—JEAN BAUDRILLARD

The powers have to be consulted again directly— again, again and again. Our primary task is to learn, not so much what they are said to have said, as how to approach them, evoke fresh speech from them, and understand that speech. In the face of such an assignment, we must all remain dilettantes, whether we like it or not.

—HEINRICH ZIMMER

He hated hearing last things. It was the breath, the quantity of oxygen in the blood. The rhetoric of the blood. It presents itself directly to the senses.

—NORMA COLE

Goddamnit, I feel like Tristan Tzara. For instance, the free patio furniture across the street has not moved for days, and I couldn't give a fuck. Every beginning is the same. All morning I hear the refrain, *Suicide slide*, from some schizometric Chalice of Then. Right. What to represent then, myself, other than, say, *the aberrancy of a noble gas*? I have no intent to memorialise any of these political programs. The unforgivable uselessness of such calculation. [Lights cigarette.] *The wave grows stronger when the wave is denied...* You could say that I indeed knew about everything that was happening as it was happening. So stop publishing me. It wouldn't matter.

It's the end of "teleology." But here we "actually" go...

Go.

Copy.

Paste.

Copy.

Paste.

Make.

Copy.

Paste.

Cut.

Paste.

Make.

Go.

***

Cue Mahler, *Symphony No. 5 (Adagietto)*. Black tar her-
oin pony preparations of the abandoned *bonne nuit* or
hot bone in the ideal flamboyance, akinetic para-dream
of boring bodies. To the angels of correction: this lost

house will blossom like a creamery in the residuum of youth, of cherry myth, that dawns in my personalised terroristic prosperity measures.

I drip into such ribald phases and can't take it back, you know? The letter of caliginous marrow abandoned in the black house or the dark bar. Praise Satan. Pure Satan. Coke in the Mapplethorpe season. Pure ballet in the paralytic symbol of self.

And I never needed ground to undo reciprocal villainy, or discover a frog, moreover. Bitter ash and guts and a twisted field of rye to habituate the baby, a secret disease that speaks to the grey maestro of manifolds. You don't know how I destroy the years in a scribbly liquidation of all that is, all that parts the word to me. The terror of night residing in its diseased electron, dumping interviews into the Elysian leotards of time: why do we hate this arm of confusion and not the Bardo? Why do we amplify patriotic dolphin farms over egalitarian slime? The good tusk andromeda crypt. That's why.

Dysthymic corn puff entourage inoculates a palindromic, Taconic pear shrift, its hands dusty like a mariachi pram. Put the littler kids in the back of the wig, strapped to the bottom of the igneous console, he imparts delightfully. It was such a way with the windshield witnesses, too. It was such a way, or something like edible talismanic jugs, scooping up pendulums, and then I walk in, and trouble stacks. It's fall. Now the faker essence unlearns to stare down a hundred airs. Raw cow sense, you know, a semblant adrenaline of water, the real coy tendency of ape stores. It goes glueing without alkaline's frustration code, or caloric theme-bobber. Right.

I go: gap, plug, zoo, grape, scion, mycelium, coptic mantle limits you seize in inbred goldmines. Dachshund trash cart or mental poison click, and what should I know about your constructive, active layerings? The minds have arrived and their spoons have forsaken them for a hundred reasons, a hundred boxes, and the roof is gone. I don't know why any of this is with and without you: it depends on the animal and how it moves with the sword's song, a scattered blemish. The hearts are medical, but the arson never goes to any of those lengths. Hellhound in the sane trees of the most important thing I've ever done, and still I wonder about you, your body, your unpacked scam cloud.

Old ocular gem with a twist of German poetry, how does my ancestor sound in his own blood? Yeah, I know. You told me that ice was love in the war for Sudanese sundown, or a carcass in the satisfied wellspring of bland coxcombs. It seems to represent something other than mouth buttons. Do we even need it? We don't.

True visible rhododendrons in the roaring quiche of ceilings, alcoholics of preponderance, bituminous cash beach, a honeycomb humps every light. Equal stares from the dirt. I've seen you in the sincere pie of sevens, as a random, loose venom emptied into watersport, hiding, falling back into an ink-filled alleyway. No names play. You've heard about circular pain, no doubt. Why didn't we, in hindsight, sample folders from the glyptic bags?

*

Some kind of ridiculous-ass ghost barber keeps accentuating the sexual name of Azerbaijan, some personal spit target encaged by today, some representative of virtual piss kits. The beauty is imaginary bite, dreaming in the pen of the oldest urban star. Offensive but vulnerable portions: what would any of this mean to the limbs of the ravagers? First, you say attacking me is a part of the glow, the possible Marxist vegetable kick-off. Second, tan fumes imitate an impoverished, sheer repertoire of illegal ferns. Third, tense ventilators profess their Octobers to be overgrown tattoos of the wind's reaction to slits. The improper engines now turn translucent.

I found dangly coupons down there, beneath the snacky sky bulb of the 7-11. It was as if sanguine México let me moan about false glances: the story behind life. Diet neutrino clashes will go on as long as noise is the intent, in this tantric armistice environment.

Don't try to fight the day; don't try to fight its secrets. Vertical mimesis drugs, and the shrimp of approval sings, "548 miles per hour," to the tune of the spirit lying. Inculcation of the throne…

"Oh no, but in persistent metals."

Bacon, eggs, and summer's phone, a building blessed by perfume, the killing of a white mare. Warehouses mutilate the sky for what it's been doing and liberate the snow from its garbage homilies. I carry the round flask of moods, being the cold ornamental cardboard and rising teflon god that I am. Burns that reposition themselves in glistening gifts. My instincts vibrate with astral claws, the wheels of life, the knees of blurry, conical vortices; life gives itself to the passwords beyond critical sand. True plagues of love, true wildcats in Floridian nights: *mutatis mutandis*, or whatever.

"Supposing that one's mind is uncovered, I pass the breathalyser its skin back. Christ is was."

Goddamnit, I feel like Wanda Coleman. Catalogues of time decked out in real penetration retainers: this is how I go about trusting the documents of glorification. Feelings are a bit of luck to the survivors of reality. Limericks of the blind, how do you guess the vocal glades of horn spigots? Crack in the sixth term, ability becomes the film in dreams; caucasians whore themselves out for blue drawings. The minutes and moments unfold beneath the shade of disbelief. My eyes are their own planets.

The body is barely ever home, betting on the rote solemnity of red check marks. I kiss the fevers; I turn inside to glean the cold calculators of waking bannisters; I hide vanity mirrors in the glossy soils of tremoring pain. Elliptical bingo cards retaliate against the agents of normalcy, and at this point I don't blame them. Life is a revolving, gelatinous leaving-off, if you know what I mean: perpendicular Boschian eyes, trivial hair corrosion.

But some things boost the moral traffic planes: some editions of coaxial, occult decibels, for instance. The invalid number of the drama curse. Equal signs propagate sleep cycles of nausea under plastic vines. Love lives in a cylindrical chandelier of disappearing clowns. You swallow the bride whole and paint huge crosses of cocaine on the bride's weeds. My mind tells me the come of of.

*

Hats take advantage of the sea and galaxy, with moaning cars full of gall and pies full of poverty.

I know of secret works ablative with supernal chemical burns. Though I still am not the radiation of fantasy's imperfect flies. All four seasons with slim to nothing while fame rises from the praying mantis of men. Shame, shame as golden alligator teeth, shame as summer sliding to the bottom in a Venusian beak. Spring laying itself down directly before a weapon of sugar. Fall drawing flapping royal bags in its endless interior, never stopping to extricate itself from the terrible addiction to hired nights. Winter cut its own throat.

"Winter, cut."

One's own throat spelling from hell boys' names in bell towers, in mushroom horror, in agony beyond drone and cash and reason. I hear mirrors begin to remember your friends. And your fate. Which is never to be away.

Bored in the cortical filing cabinet, I'll stick it out. Ducks of pleasure like a tempting, cynical siring. Come on, now.

*

Put the lid on your dark pale tale, prince. The pockets wherein we live remain defenceless. In fact, their wedding glows with weeping sails, her body is the bail and the lawn of friendship, when I see what will shuns from the mouth of fire. Bones dream too. Holy seeds excavate clones of faded waves. The voice is glowing, gay and echoless, spatial though, and trapped in pairs of pants. Wonder has floored and flavoured the vesting of imperial scares. My hand grows a flame that gorgeous lindens pray to, and we know that love singes the breast of love's ear. I'm tired of my phlegm, my gyrating all-green vacancy, my daybed of horrible curvature nonsense. Now my tears chew time through me, through grizzly and private thaumaturgy. I took the train at Kingston-Throop.

"In the full light of the world, in the full light of the world."

*

In the full light of the world, I have actively hated the isolation of signs. But I've saved many lives with such. Dark waves of prey commingle with certain sleeves of risk, playing with the works of blessed zipper beds. The light inside the skull pains me. And its 69 drugs of tormented Aprille. No one cares for the air's animal disease. Now there are pure telescopes of occluded memory, pears from purity's errors. As sure as the carpentry starts in flagrant emerald beings.

I put the groping putrescent cloak on. Oh, right, of course, the capital cape dolls also want to fight the wan version of me. The hooker stains on your deliberate clockface are flying off into time violently.

Should we have blamed a fourth of all skills for the blood of the good? Scattered pilots invade a world of new unconsciousness, and, yes, the style of my eyes is battered by tasteless murals of pain. The sane are now known as the lust of you. Redefining the world as a black daughter, I am more surgical than tidal Sufis. Just dinner pains. Just air in the waves. Just the cholesterol of death's caution. My hand is miasmic. Obsessed with prior impurity stunts. The King James Version of outer space.

"Like summer in the moth of all that replies to my certain essence, a bed in the grind gold turns away."

Certain glass punctuation desires, certain nods to the office of the untouched backward peasant; am I dreaming? Glasgow bulimia and me, and how deep is the ocean when it's barking, protected by what no one knows is going to happen. Ongoing sapphire. Guamanian vampire and metal meal. Who do you think is their guest?

Phallic Robespierre. We like menstrual cops. External vice.

Kill me, then we'll see how much the judges wane: the sun with its titillating cutlery. These are all over-the-top sauntering window slums. Back to four things though. First, telepathic windchimes excoriating Christ for his internal fiery dolphin plug. Second, homeless tapestries all unfollowed me, and I don't appreciate that. Third, detached shadow spell silk green movement. Fourth, incandescent battering rams against doors of butter. Pour me from the inside, or you don't have the chops for this.

Most happenings appear like predestined skid marks. This is what I get for helping Niagara with its epileptic belting procedure. Co-viridian night flights into aspect homes; sunlight is now considered fashion. Bodies out in the cold cocoa of delight, the hallways of birth and older types of calculus, as if Death could not book yourselves a surprise. You shouldn't slur at the boat scum. Simple diver of the fervent inhalation Cerberus, I pray for worse bird melts. I pray for knights inside of their aimless days. My shares in the kid stayed the same over four decades. A question for terrorists in a fucking enchilada.

Biblical Kirkland remains.

Painted lineament capitals.

Parodying the defeat of fundamental cashmere. My latest edition is an intro to horse stuffing, Hollywood's patterns that chiefly christen ratios of natural weather with understated form machines. The government widens when called, and it tells the dead of their prizes all the same. Incapable of sympathy in the saddle. Incapable of comprehending the duck feathers of her soul's position, in me a lake hyperventilates and boils with dolls. The lobster of summation. Holding up mansions, begging for years earlier when the shame of being an operational crucifixion pulled hate from people of the day. A late pallid goat is better than all of it. A serum, a change in actual leaves easing into dark stuff, substances that high risk de-escalated loves prepare for educational games. Higher reality gears catching blossoms by policy, by shrapnel, or cheers. Or oceanic catharsis. Ample human details winging it for balsam preparation or nepenthetic tutelage. Do you hear the rousing through May? The subcultural Hesiod of rain? Injunctions nightly shocked but twerking, roommates fighting over cinematic qi. Hash, lighting an imperial shrew.

Aliens can see you in the plagues. Sardonic shame coffee wearing a wolf's seedmind and repartee. Wearing the right-wing aspirin being alive. A gale and an arsonist, in your hook of erroneous public Portuguese warmth. Jail in the glades, fault news baking porous castle clouds. Diction at the pussy's angle. How many teeth are submerged in the spellbound Gallic barn? Hold my outer mind with weak whales and repetitive sales clowns. 4:45pm?

Foam god pointing down. Authentic mahjong. In the night of unclean time, in the day of every sand war, ministerial gland gore. I'll shine until the enzymes focus. The breath is the spending of time in a spending climate. Turning martyrs into abstract food questions. Turning agents of the scabrous blind monocle into Corsican frangibility maestros. It's all incognito dust bumps. Skymelt tenderloin proof. 1,000 proof.

*

My favourite appetite is owls, do you see now? A cage of original blue, an original blue cage, stages of impaired slurring where code words fumble. That's often true, you know, plantlife wants me, yes. I'm sitting in the interior eyeball. My import plays an overture for those constrained by larceny; I am like the virtue of being beheaded. Grey grapes, billowing filthy dishes. Friends in a grave with friends: hello.

"I definitely almost said *watch your fucking mouth*."

Take, for instance, the cheap archaeology of pants: boy, it's a sinister letter instructing you to maraud a Rauschenbergian fandango carcass. See the states administer their mustard exchange? It's all but seafoam withering communism. A stroke, a hedgerow of oral altars, prophecy in a can facilitated by lethal injection. So far, though, the directions are a Jacobean wicker preference, an intestinal, gentlemanly, insensate Cahuenga transfer for brokers. All the time I was told, especially at car shows, that the gates of marriage resumed under Kevlar echidna choice. Fully pampered for value, producing sparks of total recall.

Goddamnit, I feel like Robert Creeley. Or Robert Chester. Clear as a tesseract in waking, flamboyant as orgone fruition. I totally had to mix up my estate with whales. Riding on black bones to the static yawp field. I've seen you, percipient tea stroke, at a time when the venom of existence was aggrandised by spectral, statistical refills of aleatory purpose. Alrighty then. Let's go shopping.

Fresh horror reed. Marked incinerator of calcified shudder bulbs. Barthes would station himself at dry docks, waiting for distinct prize money parchment. What is warranted by gaskets combing over shade? Perfected dreaming cars or bottled brains for two gold vestal leaves. The first time, I had miniature eyeballs; the second time, I interjected while cruising for salt. That's art for New York City, you feel me? A patient plate of warfare: you can have it.

"Gum in the head is all I care about."

Walking with a cow-cow. Permanent blank on a lemon fire escape, parricide. Coal for flailing. Lift me up above the icy fat of my contracts. Guided packs of meat, what is wrong? Covetous beam prostate, what the fuck is wrong? Dinner in her hair, what the fuckity fuck fuck fuck? I evolve out of open mouth star castles, right. Centrist escapade, man, it's not a way to go out.

"Doing what we do, palpitating light breathing itself into smiling light. Seeds of self. Seeds of elf."

This has to do with windows during the Weimar Republic. Tender olive-green chickens, importing toxins but too many. High life and stamped out route, flummoxed by strolling orally through masked weirdos. I watched while nothing offended all the caesarian and vegetative karma clasps. Monday, or Friday, morning, only. Water from the eyes dreams at times; water points to collateral trial ranges in Africa. Substituting corn lunch like that, the stars were enmeshed in real paper bags that distracted themselves from momentous goats of light. My breath braided in the wide open. I am a door to the very yard of your drywall by the fistful. Not looking in any direction, not hurting in the pregnant information of cop cars. Bosses writhe. Nice vanity mirror.

Passive tire shunts. Who makes the guarded arts? What kind of sleight of hand takes a biscuit candle for granted? Wiggling anonymous flame, the questions remain sober, the shit of reverie as an alluring pellucid dance partner. I reach into the bucket, and little lyrics tickle negation in Song's sign.

It's a pity that triangles go uncontested in this godforsaken cat life. Don't go scavenging in dark cells, for dark cartoons. Oh cheesy snake, I dream of you again. Oh cheesy snake, instigate the curse and birth of money in my trade. Why am I forced to hear the terror of boredom? Bricks fucking each other and such.

"Not much to see at the coffin shop today, save for this crow in a field of amber crows."

Like I have a pigeon or elves, the looking imbues the air with Tylenol heights. The soul is only a guise for pain's ground. We know this. We knew this. Love doesn't arrive for just anyone in this town. Violins go off in the bomb light; I write reductionist papers about the one-way streets and the poison of intervals between melodies. All are welcome to the little goodness that titles itself *prayer's sound*. A thousand miles in the usual talk of passenger ghosts. The plain business of going ahead. Opening the jailed me in order to think of cat's bells. The glow shedding bismuth and the marks of bismuth. Life is summery sometimes.

"Yes, gases imagine things, too."

Lapis canopy cartel, do you swear the murderous pie ends in this fear? I've seen a woman build an argument around nothing. Record skips. Record ends. Side A.

*

Side A. Chet Baker and the sacred probabilities. Cue *If I Should Lose You*. Employing doom, what, are there penguins forming to deter me from their calculations? My private bone structure should be challenging enough, in this or any other room. You suck in the heart as it suck-sucks. Blowjob passing by the beginning of sleep. Never tempered for Montana like that. I'd hang on to the end of it, but the colours were a little swervy. This is all about a mellifluous abrasion cortex and nothing else.

"I want the full amount. Which, today, should be like $10,000."

You have to listen to me. Blue whales covered in glitter. A supper of ultramarine erasure. I swear to god, what steam wears might as well be blind snow. One out of five will end in flames. Professional Julissa: Julissa is a professional. Dashboard kinetics opening new accounts in the name of last things. Check the clock, tired fire hydrant. Check the cloak.

Fine, flooded heart pastes; sad gelatin notes. What do you care what hour it is? Psychosis makes you think it. Extreme codpiece surface, we have to fly out Saturday.

The point is: Time's perfect children have impregnated me. Macedonian piss pills? At the time of the tropical games, I truly felt at peace. Peepholes all wrongly filled with veal. All willpower running on off-white gloom. I feel the beginning of squealing petrol hills, emphatically things railing against gulches of shame.

Celebratory god-scry making rain in the lobbyist metropole. In my mind, sunshine moves like an Indian hidden or enshrined in silver song. Suitcases. Love as the blind stick turning around, soft and kind of on fire. Suitcases. South Carolina's womb kicks the helium saviour. Suitcases. Dark silos of holy holes. Suitcases. Butter croissants and standing around. Suitcases. The long, distant crabapple of cesium. Suitcases. Hearing me, then hearing the mayor, a wired check certified by connective tissue from the opal beings of heart monitors. Suitcases. Arctic fizz named Sharon. Suitcases.

Pervertable canopy barons win, and did you know that a throne is a maroon what? Love is a necklace with both eyes split open. A bird imagines that. What do I call you besides the caul of ghost cities and rhythms? The kilt of sorrow disembowelled by sips of nocturnal warblers. The worm is the original kicker of plasticised mouth illimitation. The notches themselves are vibratory. No candles have been replaced with water.

"Art is bottled by words in phobic order." Cha-ching.

Imperial garbage pterodactyl. Be here and be closer, agenda, my cord. This is maximum doggy bag. The whole of life weaponised like a den of cobras. Honey scowls, refusing to rise from its stars. Madness storming a trillion exoplanets. When I see the circles of the living, I evolve into the stiff campus of enemies and withered lump sprains. You would never text me anything that wasn't a saddle. How do you ram stuff into blood? We live in the frontal flailing orbit.

Disguised pentagram buttons, I will let you know as soon as the tangents of correction return. Prophesying residual four-sided cantaloupe stacks, god pursues you in the winds of methamphetamine, in the diet of pavement, breathing hollow bees, sermons arise from the chance erasure of saturnine goldmines. Lakes lay fruit in blasphemous rain. Night being ordinary rain also. Relapsing on mental ides, surefire cream atrophying like a jewel in grey totality: the right thing. Exchanges of cold world eyes deter nothing, as cures for latent knowledge decay on the symbols of day, and there are no rules to funereal palsy, especially when demeaning exits fuel nests of offal. Ignorant recipes need the sun between their knees, the right time for fucking millenial botany, aliens waving their catastrophic pencil seeds in a gorge of lavender bones. On horses in lavender rivers of beef. Violence wears the coronal drip of worth, washing angelic weeds with lasers in winter. Clothes drown, smoke fries your thighs, your apple spectrographically.

"The ground lives in me."

"Places glow with oceans of seas."

Scores of portraits rebrand the unfinished essence of thievery. Screams observe. Distant protracted verbiage, Coca-Cola, horseshoe weary, pillows dying in marshes of silence, the closeted economy, empanadas of wigs, cold weather varnishing; I walk to the wasted archer's evening dry rot. Place appears in me. Forks accumulate, appearances' breezes grieve. In Judith time, in lecherous joke praise, diamond ear seam, justice acquiring wings for free. Fugitive girth pamphlet. A Ricardo risking it all among the fringe gossamer fawns. Territory of malevolent tetra things. Gunnysack gunlight delight.

*

Perfect asshole. Debt. Laundry. Marionettes. Lamb shank. Hairball. Discus. Chamois. I'm going outside now.

Curative dictation around belts. I'm inviting you to hell by the beach. From scratch.

"Dreams that coruscate from both up close and far away…"

All the broken slut lamps, the cheetah dolls: I can see inside the body, every body, all the time. At all times. In all time. Negative and positive. Tending to be apparent in the lemonade only. There goes the Pfizer episode. For me, that equals pure folly. The last time I had chin stress, motherfuckers thought it was a birthday party. Where in the hell did you find this "I"?

I remember staying dead in the half-polemic seizure price. I mean, "piece." I mean, "peace." Pantheons arise from what we would call "ballad-tears," pleasure in the vain anarchy of summary glance. Socratic dialtones. Diet glass. Private skunk. Passionbook of barbaric censure. His dreams have been cast into the brook. Just *The Brook*. You feel it coming alive now, don't you? The voice in the ceiling's bruise. That's me. Do you feel me coming to life? I once wrote "slanted access, magnetic to nothing," and perhaps that was saying something. Clutter coded in the sable onion, the sable haberdashery, the sable laceration. I once wrote "Stanislaus Stanislavski," and others began to compete. Neglected coventry posture. Life is worth it. Life is worth life, right? Mourning is the work of spritely colour blind cokeheads, I kneel in the positivity of dream scrubs; times pass. The last movement is always seen. Seen from afar? It doesn't fucking matter.

Brilliant Corners comes on, and then "I" forget about "me."

Clattering Chaucer. Expense. Worship fatigue. Werewolf fatigue. Trigonometric pus. Seance of stairs. Desk destitution. Prostitution. Endorphin mask and brains. Two. No, three. Balkans in blue dabs. I wonder.

Multifarious wings churn prematurely. Every wing in the ear, a burning body. Cast yourself before the welfare erotic. Did you notice the beauty that transmutes the sky and its equivalent x-ray? No material. My eyes sound like a hundred suns. No material.

*

Goddamnit, I feel like Alice Rahon. Weak Victorian octagon, send me simple targets. Send me treason in the handheld portable revelator pork loin. This is distinct love obfuscation; the hex of all exonerated solipsists.

"This is distinct love obfuscation; the hex of all exonerated solipsists."

Time to test the cat lung. Time to earn the spring's dangling mystery meat. My genetic fashion-meal. You may act with the knowledge that all of life is levitating, but you'd still be wrong. All of your shit be damned.

I turn it into the perfect poem, if you do not understand. Are these Jesus's plans for the pork buns?

"The sky is getting fatter, less attractive."

The ground becomes a pornographic hole, for instance. Record that. I hear chainmail imbibing its pink, surviving through the domestic voltage experience of quiet. Pets ponder and reflect on their sports and densities.

*

What interests me is the flame in the act of sameness. What interests you is the shell of sex. The bothersome forefront of expectation-in-the-briars. Johny knows; his blood-growth portrait spells out the trained razors of the mind in the mind. Morning happiness. Quality carts at the end of life. I am not walking on glass on weekends.

The pressure has grown into stuffed belts. Impromptu true China Iroquois. I have interviewed an oscillation. It's forthcoming.

"Smoking like that in the basket of burns, man…"

The sauce of sin is an easy ear, marching among the sweet trees. Irish and cure. Wind all over the packaging tokens, solid, continual cab wheels, the caravan of sober roofs. Baphomet saviour, dance it all out. Energy would brine the hair of Oman, the cataracts of swart but glowing forms. Terrible stack-hole, iconic sea boots, I'm lying, the spells rise, Kaiserish.

A caught doll in the cast of a new one. Non-medical Euro-pro extraneous delay Cal Ripkens. I'll work for you "until the water is gone." Do you feel certifiably sad inside that meat? A blue wrong, or blue wrongs. But blue wrongs what? Schedules? Sandbags? Douchebags? Arroyos? Baku?

Ass cathedral. Circumstances beyond my blowhole. Through permanent blank indifferent forestry sites, as long as you carry clerically sudden substances of arduous longitudinal husbandry titles, the moths will scream over your unpackaged bubble wrap rolls. Comedy is as inviolable as a six-million-dollar piece of shit. The rain, hot again. The sigil: knees. Firemen are upon us, the desks will not stay abrupt. Shock pieces in their topless vinyl consciousness. I didn't know your little Santa dreams were so repetitive. That's cute.

"Air pumps young stones full of mushroom clouds."

Regular ropes all tied to the memory house. Downers. Silence inside the cape, the wondering hospital stays, the cold curtains of cigarettes dreaming, love's tongue on its own dreaming, I am embraced by the seas of Korea, John Keats, the Bible in weird carriages. Lightning knows. Skylit senators hearing honey know, the dark envelopes of innertubes know. Like ink, I've been through a gallon of mind. Rude wave pools, how could you be that young gazelle; money is strange. Sacred hair courts. Times will change the cobalt, heavenly tongues. I walk people into water past the hippo lights. Black model railroad track. Doctor of the upper wake plea. My heart is hollow; my skin waives tears.

"Aries, charts of the roach tree, breakers of the first toll booths: I was scared in the golden blue."

Adults falter in sham death, no matter what. Gloves on, please. Aqua in the middle of you two. Corporate isthmus blessing, cornish game hen of truth, belted, glommed Uruguay. Sister Joseph, the sheen recovers from the phone's universe. Ligurian where-time, autopsy of beef, Vermont Avenue, I read the diary of every caballo. Teenage fiery mulch school. Ibsen and yes. Larry's dangers. A Kenyan tooth encourages alternate Plavas; I would engorge feline tablets of weight. So listen, global outcrop of mercury trapping the dimly lit uranium. A sequel to Golgotha. Ununquadium spell, for at least I know the doors are adorable fontanelle prisms. Now.

"And everytime I do it, a colour literally canoes out of me…"

He just said it was fucking time to take it easy. Working the velocitous pelt on daze mode. Unacquainted with Upanishad Malcolms, little viruses discuss birth in a realm where vines fly. And did you even know about the hat saws? Highly bulbous. Human ham sandwich. Hanuman as a wetback or hurricane. We'll let you know.

"I'm smoking pre-rolls at the BNP Paribas Open, don't disturb me."

Keep an eye out for the shrewd grass cuttings. Don't disturb me. At the MoMA, drinking Budweiser out of a candelabra. Don't disturb me. You put your head on a terrible dollar. Don't disturb me.

Oh what do I really love? What could I really love?

*

Cue Pauline Oliveros' *I of IV*. Amazonian tits on the Shogun. As sweet as a hole in a blowsy place. Oh trash papa, a brief star wanders, methodical digital pariah. Questions assuming the night? Or beasts of practical, corporate, flowering nuns? Litigious vehicle passer, basest copulation endurer, torture is given names like Samurai. Whips, Ecuador, terrestrial haptic mimesis or koan, why do I even bother? Why do I even fucking bother?

All I will have offered are these scars to the freezing coast of memories' seams. I am not the songwriter of passive drought, I am used to the lion's round door, the unguent energy of every fin de siecle takeaway hellmouth; fall, over animosity's solid rain. Oral winter, do you get it yet? I see through synaesthetic destiny, perhaps a balance of negative fingers will numb the Orion unknown by morose farmers. Airy thing, wanting the tool of new and daunting scene fuel.

Take a stick to the doll's summer prism. Shunning yearlings for the photograph. Enemies get me in the garden strip mood, sweetly wringing paper mauve rage, in silver neck braces, in dishevelled clay cages, in the laughter of spectral entrances undivided by energy.

Little weedlets bleed out their love. Something both rude and refined, the coveted tides enflame and fracture spirits or trains. As cold and sybaritic as the sun is. Here come the big guns, the posthumous pill traps, the evanescence of Hrastnik. In this way, seeds are labial bowling trinomials, imagining Guelph as a moaning shell magnet. Everybody wants what is blaming, on the fritz. Horses are the endless poker check. Mom. *Scenic orbis.*

If you can't see a casual speech doll in the littering room, then I am sorry. I ruined the cemetery for serial kettles. They owe me a stippled sky now. Put your lovely arms in the metaphor. A guilty lip. A violent abyss.

It's beautiful, it's arrhythmic, in your heart. The quiet wonder guts, natural president, at night the clean bliss stump. And you too can be beyond elk fur. A fantasy walking. Remain in the heat, remain in the arpeggio leaps. Disconcerted white hands forage for myopic hell rims. What I'm saying is: lampposts bleed taqueria blood.

"Do you taste mouth tartare in the cloths, in the vitrine column births?"

What about the camera? What about existential cortisols? What about live irreverent steam-powered Belizean dollar metrics? What about cool vanilla suicide bombings and lambskin somatic war chests? A veritable mushroom at the gates of destiny? Pushing wan night to the brink of replication? Surrogate porridge in a craft-making mood? Dandelions that unfreeze themselves from a promenade's cabal? Surely, what about three Cartesian palm readers in general fission? What about these things? Are they merely cutlery for the unbroken ursine voice strand? Are they supposed to locate drifting macaroni? Are they fundamental hitching post liquids, returning for a sizable return on investment in their human game strings? Are vegetables swimming? Are lachrymose ass calendars in the shadows and in the way? Are they happy here, in their pen of rainbows?

"Wisdom gives off a glare of pure car crash circuity. When it glows, it glows from the death beef of kites in summer."

Goddamnit, I feel like Jean-Joseph Rabearivelo. Yes, we know: insensate leaning bondage. Supporting smithereen cocks on gossamer-bound boat joists. Fun facts grow like cheap demagogues; the heart is a part of leprechaun proof.

"Reminded of diagonal comportment; fuel bulletins parked in the fiscal truth lips. Are you prepared to take responsibility?"

*

Plural keepsake boiler rooms on the defence. We're going into the factories of demonic stress, a perfect happening implicating venereal jade up blouses. Way back like Mayakovsky, summoning head-to-head alephs and sewage stakes. Paddling carbon break. Burgundy farm cochlea within within, but as exponential praise booth, there are not years to compile. The last fire wad was a few seconds ago. Chicagoan oceans speak to the stone of carceral shimmering vacations. Puffing up emetic gems like cigarettes of sun, the blazed box of wayside ultra-waves, by twos in a tubercular cave. Too bad for the black cat's burns, enhanced by decorations like knobs on a perverted fortress of meditation. One hundred stems in the high, honeyed afternoon, worn off, continuity challenged by chalice.

There are stables that travel into your mercurial windpipe; you know that, right? The calyx of the dried out bunny. I'd have to look up all of the targets under the shadow raiment. What is space but the silence of five green arrows, peeking in the city's foreign wig morgue? Everyone, fucked on the baffling afternoon moon.

My hearing of limestone, emblazoned platonically on the deadened phalange of itself. Voltaic pastry. As soon as a scarab reminds me of physical gel, I'll evoke nothing other than vernal nepotism, with what Douglas fir do. Pious drunks opening the cup of smoke and plain flageolets. Right.

Swearing off the mottled dawn chips, once again, freezer burn and focus on a high-pitched ringing. Mongolian mud gongs: take all of your unctuous gold teeth and pray that they are never licked. Pray for the dildo darting around the pond of the stuff that's real. I'd rather rank modes than be a liberal; think about the kind coconut crops.

"It's about how vicious I could have been; if I cannot make the elephants blend, then I'll make the shit heavier."

Perhaps pass me that cartilage hat, a season of delayed teal. Midnight muffins arising out of arrears. It is chill and womanly, six times the official sport. I'm pounding hair pudding, and in front of me is a beauty I can't bludgeon. Talk about the slim animator, the dolphin giggle. Any army is for you to go to bed to. It breaks differently though, when you try to throw textual hand masks at miraculous bone ties. Hockey corn. The pitfalls, condoned by wooden eyes. But why?

Harmony. Dawn. Falling. Up in the diamond die, things are side to side.

Heaven as an animal, cause your eyes to see the palace. On a lake, riding in the peace of seeds. Now what is your t-shirt but a welcoming monstrosity, not writing to oneself, but out in the thin copper season, opal is the key to the crackhouse of my life.

Cue This Heat's *Horizontal Hold*. Diaphanous reverend spray, a quilt of exile, in national purgation. Io, how the fools add on to their cheekless whimper.

Cackling privacy with two schools of indigo. Never mind the decoration of seconds, the vicissitudes of select rejuvenation parts. It's in you: the no mass.

Bike parts in a feather ring. You are this desk, this deep sea suicide. Cancelling four Xaviers, sand will survive though inert and suppressed. Puffin extraction. Bye melts in the tin foil ceremony, the godless head binding where normal texts are revived by El Monarca. Lusting revolver, addendums for a saboteur's drive, slick car boil. Bah. Alternating consequences. Do you feel the unthreading?

The art of lurking in Alhambra. The satyrs of water's fighting and melding. Incessant miasma and vaudeville science. Vapour isolating hairy pastures of something medical, cement, or ancestral. Dedicated to pressure rings in the liquid nocturnal. The shuffle that burns each victimised corsage volt. Traitorous fan belt tensions and the like. Try being gone so long that your vascular mothers advance and arrive after you into the antecedent "No."

Try it.

No, for real, try it.

*

Eggs of long, derivative slave-ship-type-of-finance, just keep walking. A course of everything you see, the raw, the white-gold *sangre* breath, gel flocks of eternal pachyderms, the movie ends with heliocentrism replacing the theocratic topography of *die Drehtüren*. Unadulterated poltergeist scores come this way, moulting critical pyramids in so many casuist ways. The dark firecracker.

The bland male pool and what the winter winds scheme, anonymous and creamy mosques, a rented Earth for all of the batchelor hate: my dreams curve out of the heart smashed open. It is like a nude wet spin, a silicone laugh without hearing any iridescence. My, my, my, the screeching is thick with shadows, or sharks, or... colourless gaps? Only local mothers thin out their owls.

A can of paint rises from the wine, demon. Cadaverous maw of sundry blue rinsing fats.

The sediments leave me speaking of burns. Oh yeah, the banana tree burns, the red eye of lacking oxygen, the burns from that, the burns from gunpowder roaches on a skeleton, basalt burns on the dislocated shoulder, theatrical burns from the oasis of paratroopers. Nuptial clones reverse their bedpans. End of story.

But also, not the end of the story, of course. Of course, c'mon.

*

"Thigh bones, their metrical scurrying, and my blotted out canvas of car-green war crimes; nothing is the same."

Carnelian vines. My kinship only ignites with the tender, aware of psychic dalmatians, getting off the bridge with my son, I will continue to portray the art of calm glue. Dishonesty will sever the sun's glands from the violet tide. The day is deaf, the hamburgers at rest. A big C teleports from 8th grade to time's red. The levitation is fine. That's what I call narcoleptic pre-bones.

Insidious landscape fingering. Tendrils entertain the terror of the abstract. Have I said that before? Feels like it. Recovery strippers on the tiles outcrop of place. Lizard scream, cold in the hymen or summer light.

Try a way to purely pimp it. The bubble tree is the source, the decapitated centre redacts us. But my force is the ocular oil of the world, the Budapest soft dream of Italian hermitage. You see pictures, but you don't know what their weight is. Something you will never defend.

I may need the world to cooperate with skeletons. I don't know yet. The green fountains of life are indistinct from possibility. A slow scattering of liars: that the dream is on the brink of a coda? Partners who accentuate prayers for each other, somehow richness implants itself in the negative flight frame.

"Passion for a horsey nemesis debacle in which your uteruses subscribe to coughing up cash power."

Nature calibrating imbrication. No matter, thieves stab me in the back of my hair. It's a question of Sprite and mosquito masks, the ruining of 100 milk burials. Implicit serial hats, we don't agree on everything. Unless, of course, the rye is in the squirrel. Put your hands together: nobody is going to say anything. I can't believe you blew the secret eyelid off a golden owl. There is nothing as wicked as firstborn wood.

Cue Cecil Taylor's *Conquistador*. The red centrefold of Death's pantry: gods unguarded by chains of birth, unbelievable sea view, grotesque planet of hours in stained glass. Further mandrake meditating, or not. Further pursuing the moon's electrocution, or not. I don't care. There are zero others who burrow as worms above the dumbness of time. I exude four hearts for every one of yours.

Make way for the tiny mute glancer of Oulipian prayers. Make way for fire on a stairwell of fire in a world without a face. Make way for the clover which has come so far from the pallbearers' parade. Make way for the dumb tubes of easy-come-easy-go. Do I love you? Yes, I love you.

"There is a project older to the lungs than is."

On you there are overt-in-death seas and ridiculed and impassioned by the separation of stripes. There exist no audible reversion rackets. No tin passports for the madrigal's toilet dame.

Goddamnit, I feel like Unica Zürn. An African trage-dian mulling over person-drop soup. Sundials of corn in glory, in suits, or parts of vehicular regal semaphore.

I rap in the wine-green riot door, circling clandestine mitre balloons for the sheer joy of interceding. You'll feel good about that, won't you? What do you say?

Keep the snow inside the vines. The Zamzam faxing itself to China. I don't want to get there, and then all of a sudden I'm confronted by a violent cat-shark.

Defining your moth blessings as twin stitches of the broken freighter. Make a cracker turn around.

Scapular hulk party, frenetic lead blaze in a wheelchair. Space as fancy, wobbling, leathern eyes in pairs and pairs, leaving subtext in the oldest glass. My melting world of cheetahs within stares, a bus of bitumen or a candle sliding through the skull of an off-white rat. These things have been turned to ash. These things are ash. Little trapdoors of violence, do you speak to each other in the way cold cousins do? Nepenthean crime slab, you have the childish eyes of an other seeing. The inherent crabs of doubt are shut out too. So fucking purple: the world as a mental ogre.

I knew a calendar that sat upon the elegance of patriarchs. Unbelievable poor chassis of blank embitterment, my succumbence is the blatant winter. The naked hole knows what I'm talking about. I would be a fabular table upon nullified greatness and low-brow conscience jewels. Have you run out of druidic bowling subs?

"We need the drama to be simple; animals applying various schools of bland shade, juice in their eyes."

*

To begin again.

Go.

Make.

Look at this little fascination with views. What else could one want beyond misguided lunch. Time in Spain? Obeying the clock? Balaclava? Hate? Shapes of death? Kooky planets? Well, my plans have unfolded like the fool I am.

As a rabbit, I shamed myself into foraging for seeds. The rabbit itself was a circle. Pain became another one. Golden hours showed me how to count and bless hexagons with definition, to grasp the chips of the ground and send them to their proper districts. I called this *excellence*.

But what should I do now, now that red groynes unfold by forking, loving levers seemingly touched by two moons, distinctive in their song pleasures?

I can do it without forcing the value from unfinished wolves; a man could turn all of this off. And still have California on the tongue. Ow.

Goddamnit, I'm André Breton. My blood has been described as a beautiful corny crest. Because I lean into the form of form. Reality has no right to place stars on top of this place, I say to all virgins. A customer inhabits everyone I see. Catch my talented gall?

A can of spring in the orthotic time of retrospection. My nuns behold roaming blunts. You'll never find your way back to the brink of blanket sap.

Iraqi summary sand begins to shine; blocks of the lizard social system blessed by the picnics of thin words. My spit comes in clinics, if you don't drink from withered bosoms. Islands shiver. What to do with all of these premonitions at the wrong end of a microscope...

More is present than could be assumed by the snooping tit cradle. A very peerless knowing, little drudgery so fearsome in its bedroom notes. Play on.

Cue Steve Reich's *Come Out*. Tripped-out medical t-shirts enter the fray. Pharmacies become dispersed by actual movement; cubes aligned in the nothingness of snow. Precious nonsense grows in the chewing meat or atomised true ice. Even the grave pirates of the sun can climb night's call, which induces no controversy whatsoever.

"Unloyal hours, the cafe of quitting salvation sequences begins with breath in windshields of sleep."

I see the dark in L.A. I see the pills boarding boats beneath the waves, time-cold wobbles until secret backpacks find the moon and its empty dreams of a theremin. God-stress turning wombs to sidewalk scrubs, every day bleating, runways with hateful llamas growing bruise-blue. Talkative algebra, tell me about death, tell me about your bedroom, every channel showing visceral teeth and ribbons of self, being sued by the rain for wondering slits. Take. Take. Take.

The alto appearance of light is scathing, a dream broth that takes poor Knights Templar to the curves of mansions and whistles. A mudra commingling with a murderess and her ninnies. Like lava in the oceans of humidifiers, like a turning pageant of roars, the star descends from vertigo, from veracity on to cage a calorie. A flame for the disarmed and disembowelled.

What is the highly visible but muted mouth of now? A trickled wish? Someone's covering of stock?

Subjects in the organised thoughts of massive purple. Irregular shoguns launching this. Neptune Scorpio prone. The poorly designed impulse jungle, resting on immanent pleas of occasion. Crosses blown-out by you and me: I feel a whisper taunting aerospace boom priors.

"Acolytes of the saurian moon begin their caffeinated piracy submersion, their effloresced gang trail which revives nails and the bloody word."

Mama had a hug-coloured shoe. The body as resuscitated nuclear dime. The growing maturation spoon principle, or so it seems, but also sublime, critical cash wives, and then there are supine glimmering restrooms. But the *was* doesn't know what the face was. Minuscule neutered calcium, ok. Say something else.

Orphans paint the eyes and nose from tin cans. Cyan escapes from the trusty oak pole, and that's the sky blue sum of side-splitting luck, or graves. I made a stop in Saginaw to attend the parlour game of ingrates. Chewing tenebrous boats and their plump clockwork gourds. The doing is in the emptying.

I'll liquefy beasts in my own mind. Claiming old ghosts as speed vests, muttering grey steerage afloat in the mirrored bog. The flack is bunned this day; how does it work? The madam is hell, the Bronx too.

"But never mind: the castle can't tell parasites from freshly shorn breeding tents, god's wreck from shabby emeralds, wet sticks from gift receipts..."

Goddamnit, I feel like Laurence Weisberg. We haven't got any bread; we haven't got any death prose. Glowing wand dinner, light-coloured stones playing with their breasts. Time has found new legs underground, and no one expected that. Traffic goats, too, want a loan from steel mavens, as they're running late with skids, slowly negating prayer's bones.

Goodnight, sensual lepers! Goodnight, golden whorehouse! Goodnight, trampoline gap! Goodnight, gunclad wheelbarrow beside the white poets! Goodnight,

jailbait Gemini! Goodnight! Goodnight, epic pre-
dation sandwich! Goodnight, jukebox slayer! Goodnight, perverted rattler of the stated duende branch!
Goodnight! Goodnight, glow of bloated wombats!
Goodnight, pinstripe pelvic ring! Goodnight, fruit-
cake of bureaucratic nightmares! Goodnight! See you
tomorrow! Goodnight!

*

It wasn't all soup and starvation.

"Consider my death the cusp of the boring body."

In many respects: ambidextrous church fire, washed
up on the back of a solar goat. Rice vest. A shiny victim
pulling head lice out of diamonds, this is how night
simplifies my nerves. Citrus and concrete rippers, a
city inert. Blind circles intersecting with an animal
sheen, in the circuitous adrenal renaissance. The sane
for higher Urizen favouritism. Surfactants in German
corners of eyes. The world on a slope of black guns,
the turning howl of the seraphic real. Discrete pussy,
discrete fly fishing, I say these things all the time, the
jewels unresponsive to heat, relentless heat, even, the *I*
unseated by veritable unconscious ovaries.

Grape Styx, water alone hides in the castle of Albanian sun. Eukaryotic dust war, find the scent of anything at war, seriously, move into the artistic gnome. Precipitous story, the word begins in the truest hyena. Ostentatious, to meet her, the fire first in all of America, thank you. All of us have been out in vans, driven to the rostrum of anywhere. I lose the done. And when I mount it all, there is a tenseness ensconced in my friend athletes. I want it all. Talking with crisp words out of my lame outlook. "The world is over 200 countries blessed by the colours of humanity." Sad knowledge, my real hall of beginning. May I demand the loose administration?

A shop is a true Maastricht. I stay off my nights, preparing for opulent transmission. My eyes have gone before me. That's called private equity. Thessaloniki holds the semaphore.

A time beginner, led to the tomb running in atriums of limps that have to be. My Holy Cup cup.

Life is the horny entrance, untouched by fervour. The second following is the flower of understanding, my *someone different* abreast of turns and wives. Here is the kind, the stygian cough. Honey points:

the cock is free. Now becomes the problem. My eyes are beknighted by clusters or mainstream evolutions.

Goddamnit, I feel like Amelia Rosselli. I mean, Amiri Baraka. But he's off into the solar labour of the dice. The journal, an agony of contradictory planets, in which the implication of French baptisement persists. It's all gone. The notes were made of pumice.

"The god-slums are for me?"

And the golden song of miscreation. It has something to do with shame, and now I'm going to get all of this disrespect out of my case. The poets move the river. Sinful dune. Pataphysical mood. Labial contour. Fiction on a bloody page, almost continual with image. A marauder of informed diving skills, the book and the sketch being one in grace. A sort of unfailing nude reader. A rapturous mid-vision gaslighting. If I had to just live a life and move through typescripts, then why is it quiet around the stark centrepiece of drugs? You can inner.

You're expecting people to burst through low-pressure poetics. These are stories in the pus of belief; I don't know how long you're allowed to ask about them. Hell points to the nigrescent river, a trout of experience transformed into a title of joy in vision. You came into time with that feeling. I mean, I came into time with that feeling.

Scrambling blood from lungs that see.

*

I mean, I used to be a dead flammerole. With the court sustaining my erectile waxen kick. I used to blame the purity of Marches.

Blackouts seriously condensed into mauve. Tertiary urging of the Tibetan skeleton, the blank Electras of slave-driving, crooked calendars aestheticise all over the city. Malleable verses of stallions glowering among bamboo. In my arch-hat of spirit death, in my cold clutch of slut brains.

The extremest pet of a lapidary day glow; drifting on monuments of boring Doric columns.

Goddamnit, I feel like Ronnie Burk (when he felt like Alejandra Pizarnik). For dirty ($) hours, my heart-beat remains unoriginal. The world is a part of its own atramentous sunlight, coiled book of the West. A thief's life: aid or tail. Doing everything I've ever

done. Cognitive breastfeeding, Mesopotamian behind enemy lines to remarkable courts of bloodletting
catamarans. There is no harm in the addict of watery
sevens. Restricting your breathing to your innards,
your measly breathspin, breathmapping. Organ aspic
of changed hats, the order of such technique.

And this is the proof of night, definite singeing of the
bonus me, on the blessed breast of everything that
doesn't love. Racism intensifies. Looking at your voic-
es as the ballast of escape, intensifies. "Overt sea-be-
ings and perpendicular clowns," intensifies, and how
would you react to that?

"You can't see the sea fumes from here, you know?"

I heard a stage was the same as a camel, you know?
Really big, fortuitous tears. Brains marked in the main
aperture of the forest. In case you wanted to know,
things went black in the bray, back in the noodling
season. I set the door grease for Cyprus, you know?

You know, just twisting this thing into Nordic pressure coats. Non-clandestine heroine. Horse towers
taken down and toured, yes, it is like that. Oh, glam-
our stall, oh, fish bracelet of tears, of years of tears.

Where does the mind not spray its panoramic heiress coat? The scent of a bone doll, many people and their commas falling into blended London, this action is assigned to no beach, a scintilla of flame and Nigerian despot.

"I brush the hair of the zoo and pain's young lesbian listens to me."

Aligning a devil's unaligned savagery protagonist with already disrespect, the scoff is for poor people in trunks, demonically serial like wonder eyes. Oh my god Australia in the veins, smell the Caesarian air? Vegetable erasure in an insane number but sounding fucking sane. And. And. You wandered into the wheel of Nazareth, probably, lady, getting two-faced so you can be trained in the curvable thunder slink.

Goddamnit, I feel like Sir Philip Sidney. Do you feel the Aegean dent of the super white world, the laundry that kills? Space as mortuary for full bags of silence, dreaming and saying that you are dreaming in the dream, to be a private person, a person who likes aeroplanes, and pancakes. All of it is cyclonically falling asleep. All of this unsure acorn, different in the self than I would be.

Days are not the same. This is the swiping of the graphic veil, a governor's core brain. But just give me a ride to the airport. I'm not trying to comb anyone's hair anymore.

*

How about the tearaway staircase? I have to step into the masked porn memory, thunder beneath the fat gasps. Hard for me to conceptualise the stomach from what smokes on the distant tubes, blessed by a levitating seal of filth. What sort of felt are you on?

The carpenter and Uncle Tellurian laugh after someone tells them they should be holding on. The aspirations of strangers, and I am not sure but the odd is kind of an adventure? We'll see. Eat the dead. Stiffless glass knife, where do you go when the portal sounds empty? We'll see. While the aqua lamp flared, gimp dragging gimp to intention, a sovereign sleep packet helped with the live concert tune called *how have you not died yet*. You will never spray batter with me, will you? We'll see. This one had hammers, a cooking leaf, and undressed collage; why don't you test my money? We'll see.

"Close crack loss over impaled dark ports, inveigled art chart from the fury of the simplest brush."

Quartz in my lair, a barrier of ingredients, I only need three minutes to get ready. You do this to us, and it's suicidal coquetry. I may just pull the French carpet to the side and take it from there. But the minute I do that I might as well wander through Amish snow. What severs the dying from the dead, mutual reconnaissance as pilgrims' technological suffering. Omens have breached all of us.

The head apart from receipts, ocular savoy summoning portraits of gold love. Gold love. You know, near the paroxysm of my leg as glottal car, brides dance equally with citizens under fire, stars burst into actual flame right above scientific silence. A morose speculum of red dreams, wet hair, bursting squirrels beneath sand, lead bedlam of lobsters, horticultural kite drip for the weather's peach neck: I imbibe this. Sumerian cream dreidel. Porous Kyrgyzstan forgery pests. A gun race, into sluices of pararhyme. No other way. No other material.

Goddamnit, I feel like Julia Ferrer. Or her physical scenery jeans on some tranquil larval bone. Or the swan of dying, windmill-white, arch-phoney. Holy slack of corrosion, match your boy in the deep-sea leopard tone.

See the sill burnt on riling? A criminal parchment blurred to scold such enamoured yesmen. Until the why-cold, the fated and unshrined apple bowl, comes with graphic laces to repair the fat clothes. Just trying. I lack a razor's tour and my circular varsity stub. You couldn't trade off drool in here, it means the spiritual is finished in deformity. And deformity.

*

"1998," let me hear you say it. Until you've fallen into the sirloin. Like a cloud arranging milkfaces around a silurian haircut, the nine hospitals fit to the portal of fresh gaiety. The foreign includes chemical tournaments for jungle… Nevermind, I watched the scalpers eat pies of love. The chapel beauty, the chapel beauty, where does she simply ride the New? It's tomorrow. It's tomorrow, when the calculators will summon Magog. When the elevators enter black camouflage dreams.

Volumes of make-believe stones clap; you're fused to Italian death markets, all you want. I feel no silhouette in this big solar chair, but basically, it is time to slay the plausible, such a rain dwarfs itself and remains breathing, cat water.

There was a sort of livid gift working with the mysterious, irresistible meat plough; the blessed cartel fixtures in their manmade wells prepare haloes of sibylline aversion. The appointment is as serious as a star. Oculus mantra, if you want to stare at the beauty hatcher, it's your mouth that does the staring, so what do you think? Do you think that we're alive?

The vault in the bathroom spritzes the fastest delayed cakes, in my certain bubble a prong of 100,000 ampules manoeuvring; I'll never stop letting it happen that way. You say your crusade is about sawing yourself in half, that's the finest kernel of thirst and beauty. The lampblack colonial page constructed of gorgeous poverty. The grand self physically borrowing from unfinished bliss. The green spoons of demoralised intellectuals. I earned a living, I secured a banal culture, and I disciplined others in a pattern of fantasy alone. It so happens that much marsupial is contrapuntal. By that I mean I've adapted to the closed-casket Bedouin presumption. Feeling inward for the thousand shapes of Prague, over roofs of orbital reality and megafauna, monarch butterflies made of skin. The whole wind being reasonable with trespass.

"If I have to learn about what festival of doors has been cast out into the hearing praise of disorder." Say it and find out why not.

*

Altitude, tonal leaves, *chaudière* of paraffin speech cousins, I give no ox no sea, a quiet tedium of Kierkegaards. Miraculous crotch play. Sabbath on a demon's dinner plate. Shooting sheep at the cinnamon limit, seeing the source of the violet matter; symbolic metals of the chronic model. Sometimes the boring are the most blessed.

Goddamnit, I feel like Osvaldo Lamborghini. Acrid fuselage. No retainer on the barn breasts. Why have the weddings, the amount of hair children, reappeared? Out of a class of the Real, jackets jacketing islands unwound by serpentiform pouches. The Real hits. It figures out the median mirror I am. Unending water on my duck. My life like the sunlit ecclesiastical carpet drip. The moon's bloodthirsty blob of decoded peacock satrap or seventeen Sundays. The rest of this idea-vine accelerates from clean lavender and salmon-coloured stockings. Good grief.

The punch-up voltage, the air without anchor of windows, shiny. Testing for a colony of flesh, the motor speedway of hell, again, almost with a missile of that Jurassic power. Hardly entry into the somnific house, to display and to devour, a field of aspersion weans from self-acumen. No, that is not the flesh. No, that is not my temper in the days of ataxia.

Cue the animal drifting over the sun. Cue the bucket-hearts in the macula of gnostic thievery. Cue the fruit fly's wing. Oh shit, can you fasten what you have tossed to the renegade whisper here, springing this growing anti-divine ghost rack? What about the normal bottom? Uncoupled columns of tar. Synthetic arc rip, never play the dumb cerulean tourist leap, over the scrambling head rows, the filthy clock couch where heroes cause tides. Everybody drops the eagle.

Two days left, leave them plastic. My eye is the siren of life. For me, the sheer vacuum of what's at stake opens the unglow. A mirror trapped in a party of Derridean nexuses. Purity shines its short occupied cicatrix. Four jet-black pages denied in the crazy word of Call. Crack rocks are actually all of the above in a fortified pork trait.

Again, financial oil in the detritus, a mariner's rain in clear wings of dawn, the presidential light fault. But do you still love me in this paradise of stares? Do you fall from the quiet opera of polemical prunes? Free speech sonogram, nightskin tearing at these sudden deserts, monarchally. 100 years of boring dust fastened to the bone of a vacant sea.

"The gold remains at eye level, masquerading as a dark night of day. The name of your city is the name of nature, its sizable letters slapped into fame."

Couldn't feel copper, everything a little more positive. Caricatures from a barbaric can. No finch, no slovenly move into past dollars. Negative now. Sloe Gin Beach inhaling us, with each transaction resulting, in methadone sense, in calm conniving, red as a kind ultra colour thinking beyond spoliated breakfast. In our alleged precursory sonar, cotton writes above clits. Ghoul of aspiring seeds, how vowel, how carceral is the dung, on a wealthy vowel path. Morass and carcass as potentially dethroned and exquisite holding names.

"Does it sound like it works in the goddamn districts? Sable light, crocus of exsanguination patterns, let the iceberg grow an egg called *The Good News II*."

Look at me, I'm a god from your better life. Goofy, and yet, horrific, escarpment.

Appalachian shield, star burial. These are nature's thoughts, and I hate nature. Loving on some murmuring, to address the rose as if it puked a phonebooth, charged for reasons tender and months of truth.

Those are those and these are these, and sometimes I drift into Blakean tri-nightmare sleep. We all live in St. Petersburg's bummish, missing document alcove, hissing at a full Colombian golem, soon I'll have the teeth of death, which lie to you, they say they'll die and then they wait for you to leave. Hot, wet, cellular. Within the play door of jade philology, it was a good day, the name of the illusion was January's Garden; she was in love with the night that would sleep with her.

"Role-bile."

Attendant Miriams. Right, subterfuge for naked negatives. Right, of every voice you should know its emptying out stage called "The Buffalo." Right, very smooth transparent snake in sudden Rome. Right, according to my notes: nocturnal emission. Right, I have a plain scalp as emotive as the delicious zoo, the irony of the mailbox, giving a year, see me among my visions, lacking motion. Right, my parking lot bonnet or religious procedural silkworms. Right. Too much drippy on the clothespins, too much loss and cylindrical misappropriation. Right, it smoothes out the head, the head of the Jess club. Right, look at the wolf in its grass cube. Right, goddamnit, I feel like Angelamaría Dávila. Right, sweetheart, my eyes are caned in the five show. Right, frangible and slapped at the terminus, I never should have learned about betta fish. Right, revised gamelan of public holiday shame, my feelings are the opposite of a real reaction. Right, narwhal natural in the tempest sheath, spirit of two Clevelands, a vandalization, monsieur, sets the air equipment on the right path. Right, benthic lapse on tape, monotonous hell craft surviving on carnival pot. Right, we have no choice but to mention three fibres asleep in the nasty noir of a happy hour bush. Right, I don't know what is hybridised within me, hanging from amoebic peace, a recipe for alternate oceans. Right, erotic relish ducts where texts go to die, where the inevitable gas landscape sparkles as supercontinent. Right, *here's the key*, said the lover to his portrait, I've been faced with candles before in dreams, this time they are sputtering the word *corn* in the kitchen. Right, a common brain straight up spoiled in the cool earth, in a barrel of games. Right, who sings to the baby its education.

Right, the unbecoming book felt as dead as the stairs, the darkened extravagant dick learning to speak of crystals. Right, vivid chain and flag of chasms, make your life backward in my heart, shape the numinous goats to your name, to my name, for the small knife that awaits every fable. Right, time is at the beginning of the cow, like a silent mountain saint, close to the leaf chair. Right, a cycle of feeling avoidance or its mechanism, I remember now, *I am interesting*.

*

"Live with me in the woodshed."

Sacrosanct as pessimist's gold, nothing is beyond my job now that I have stood up on all five sides. So, no, don't pull out the cold kit yet.

I'm going to go eat some dogs.

*

What does one really mean by the phrase *morning hamper*? I never want to talk about the flora of operations again. Chiefly negative insides, as one put drunk into the punchbowl, investing in spirituals music. Help me with the floor path, for there used to be a lunch of us doing Bible stunts.

"Do you hear me in the seraphic silence of all hearing?"

Meet the purple explainer, and then you can film me. Introducing poems of numb survival. The great accurate bodily flash, a lover torn up by lanes of money, asking for simplicity from transgression, etcetera, on the wander, eventually the end honours the ground. According to the porous, the emotion, the hair pulled, according to trigonometric nuts, the variance is slick with quiet, everyone's last name is freed from jazz rooms, appearing to be on some anal cusp. Am I you?

Remember: I was at the fractured linden. Dealing stellar steaks. Like a retarded larkspur, I leave home in a sheen of tesselated terrestrial harm, the spice of the senate indeed travels to additional autocrats in colourful spit. Only sophisticated and knocked loose on the medical bridge, the sky-fucking cyanide. Electric mattress whispering to the human ball: *space locked in the ear*. The country is not, uh, the covenant. And due to the devastation of your outcomes, it is so blackened in the shrine these days. Extraordinary.

An afternoon vessel recording a hard charge to the argon, step four includes Venezuela waiting to speak, in plain displacement mode, embarrassed. *Hold me, honey*, something about sitting near this tree or that one, and the whites have failed me once again. No famous nourishing carpentry, no Horus, no forced prison, sounds as attractive as *forever*, the garment slug of proverbial appeals.

Unsuitable blind grub, your sexual revolution saving only ache and alimony, a call to bind with the techniques of synthetic Góngoras. What do you feel? Legion? Illegal doom palettes? Cold vine blossom? God in the single clown cause? Why should one fixate on the sterling hymen? You know it's going to come with a Lemurian check, the physical armour blends, or the start of sawing somebody. The entire world wants to test me.

And goddamnit, I feel like Sebastián Salazar Bondy. Like Saddam Hussein. They say variations on perfection, the people-poets of the time, sorry for the silence a long time ago to you, sorry for the stratagems of decrucifiction. It's always about the manner of the war and two eyes. The contrary running of substance in and out of things. Things? I'm sorry for all of it. The lightning bolt rhetoric of children comes from the slain who sonorously conspire as one monstrosity. The vast thinking over geometry's power, the Architectonic Groom whose god is a blind stone. When you enter you call it a sick bath, when you arrive: the mortal speech chair, an action of the volatile spirit sleeve, the *equisitofor*, glady surfing on an apple, on a tomato of centuries. The third partner always challenges their perception of the real, they're all tellers here, in the web prism of forced company and doll response. A plate of raw cartographer in undulance. Sparkling vein. Squeezing the tip of your name out on death-day. Folder's dead. Take care of the cold cat blear. The escrow peace, a balance of Jainist Schopenhauers. It puzzles me, but I killed the leafblower. Untrue traveller of green, realistically, bottomless breast-tree of *voir*. What to cut, and what to pursue in the glaze?

I know who should venerate the sands of Appraisal Beach. Inside the refrigerated April tasks, minimal dada kingdom internal style, heartbeat one invokes by damn scheduled thud. You don't have to say circular ocean tongue, for instance. It's a gleam planet. Too many fathers underway, too many fathers you've lost in the capital of *Fern*.

Whose skin would comprehend me? Barbara Portugal in the penny ante refill armoury, and Oakland went down after snow taxes. A life of venomous faculties. Revenge is always too soon. Vertiginous cake zoot, and now true weapons, now in the payroll rhizome, now in the fresh homemade misanthropic bread pan, now you know what, nothing is surfing the slur. *What, stand up and move to the side or something?*

"The animal winds of Do Not Enter, the inadequate train."

I suppose the violence of the natural spring pill; I segregate misshapen vitiations for dominance. I may be collateral to something older than the visible evolution of percipience. Clearly in the bedpan's purity pearl, what's going around, waiting for the alarms to pay dust. Beast of the innermost timepiece, the serenaded carpet funnel, the Che Guevara fax furlough, the predated fax works, incognito shade Tennyson, it's like that. What is a green plant?

"Typeface like a water-lung. March of the horse-filled predicate. Don't get the candle for porn."

Big wig on the apricot, or prove it hard on the rectal pear. An actor is too young to die here, a dropped dread of light, and the rest believe in it. Attempting a blaze would not be in one's public favour. A real girl, a well of creamed corn, our house in pensive winds, the violence of which stays on for four or five weeks, a normal viral whippoorwill record. An open echo-gleam, a shoulder focused on the black needle of Nacogdoches. Where all of the quartiers meet, California rolls screwing each other in a capital RIGHT NOW. A mood, hehe. No material: everyday is an imperial beauty becoming even more beautiful. Why do you think your hair has come unpurpled?

Such dredge smoking in the open Heideggerian high-rises, latrines of format unfair with half-lists improperly prismed for snatching rooms. Cops are golden seers in the fitness of this drizzle; acclimated brain sea where do you fire your quiescence? Smart arm-saw floating in the slaw flurry, I'm here. I'm here gardening entrails of bothered epochal Chagalls. Draining the wall. Mating riots in a golf ball, good afternoon, mitre. A lobster pointing at strictly untrained mats, such long dead seats in a volcano. April will be brand new. A new Paraclete inside the verse.

Follicle arrangements. Goddamnit, I feel like Remedios Varo. Hundreds of hues inviting a stick to the coma bond. This is no one: a sweet passion bowl. My eyes are rotten rocks of tonelessness. Oak deformed, and who are you as loved?

Let me go get the blue table of carnations that only begin. Secular, savage, virtual, the gloss follows entire speeches of wound and strawberry. Winter fucks all of its awards, its Armenian scars, the shine of the creator in word-death. Foreign ambulances bathe in their ochre appearance of goodness. Don't you know there are years of me, lonely, dead, and light along the roach trail.

The feeling is to blame. I was not invited to the vocal levees, burning their silent weak bird burdens to cut morning like grey seeds of future travel. Did I die in the treatment plant? What about the vandals spelling out waves of extraterrestrial sin, where do the clothes within live if roses can't even cut the woollen sky as a nude owl as a skilled self-cell, as a disguise in the roster of frenetic cul-de-sacs. Why?

In here, there is no reason to hear the whole, the secrets of the golden noun, the little precipices over inviolable gumdrops. Hide the comet. The gnashing was clean, washed liver sea poised in the possible, which subtracts fire from exile, getting a glare off the condescending chest drink. As you know my car corresponds to bludgeoning, slow sincerity, cooked on the outside, no placemats, no eyes inside the acrimonious interzone. Maybe the weird drugs will sign off on layers of inosculated pains, the whipping hours of ordinary women. The heavy weird drugs of sanitation living out their truths. I can see the muse in me demand the salt in me, and I see myself living again as pure summer, pure arcane apoplexy. All that.

"Biology, or as others call it, no phonemes for the vagrant."

May I present to you: all the things outside. May I present to you: necrotic De Stijl mania. May I present to you: peach plum pussy pie alabaster sands of eternal surgery. May I present to you: the factory brings out pretend balloons. May I present to you: hypercolour feral atonement blazons. May I present to you: piranhas trapped in piranhas. May I present to you: Cycladic sweet paper and a living corpse. May I present to you: unquantifiable privates of the space within false poems. May I present to you: the constant *Zeitstelle* whose hands will fall like fruit from a beautiful fizzing illusion. May I present to you: separate cliffs for murdering the orator on the red side of direction. May I present to you: the passive triplets of obsolete and saturated glyphs. May I present to you: occult sensation of the sweaty morning design. May I present to you: chapters which read as new weeping roses. May I present to you: ascetic miscreation of brides and chaos. May I present to you: the angel of infinite and asemic

You, or mimetic splashing knife. May I present to you: crimes of landscape and unplanned birthday ripple.

"Left lane must exit."

Mythic white-arm morphine. Explicit crumbling image of ocelot. Dithyramb of purebred nonconformity.

Goddamnit, I feel like Julien Torma.

***

Now, here is something else, where I talk about the plain version of what I wanted to say. I had walked away because my growth was interrupted: the poems, the stones, had increased, but perhaps nothing but separation accompanied the mess. Perhaps the day is just beginning, unfurling its radial carnage onto the presence of things. Things. A butchered blue fur. A vertical child of Earth. And I say *let go*, and you say *it is too early*, and I say that I'm appearing in the middle of a *film noir* and am the literal book. Manifestations of one's own body are of such knowing that they can portion out the darkness of their initiation to change the still rich world. And to think I could have translated all of this as *the stone grows and is not wrong.*

79

I don't know if you've ever heard The Night before, but it talks by position and rules by beverage, I mean *severance*, I mean *poison*, I mean *semblance*, I mean *prism*, I mean *insemination*, with its pyramid of life-times in the middle of a sentence.

***

Go.

Copy.

Paste.

Copy.

Paste.

Make.

Copy.

Paste.

Cut.

Paste.

Make.

Go.

Goddamnit, I outdid RImBaud. Double Johnnie Walker Black, neat, bank account on overdraft. The free firewood across the street has not moved for days, and the wind slides into the pleasure of its ongoing pain. All endings are the same. [Stubs out cigarette on porch steps.] *Airborne snails.* How else did you expect this to go? Well, your boy's gone off to war.

All morning I hear, *Drink the dark bird of normality, Michael.* Which is not my name. The end.

"But the end is not the end."

October 2020 – August 2022
Los Angeles

Acknowledgments

Excerpts from this book first appeared in *Caesura* and *Vestiges*.

Respect and gratitude to Pablo Lopez for his invaluable critique of the early manuscript.

Peace to the co-founder of Nomaterialism, Michael Keenan.

May my friends know endurance when faced with danger, illness, and desolation.

And may my enemies remain apart from beauty.

A million blessings to JDF for having the audacity to publish this book.

Adoration to my wife and sons. I live for you.

About the author

LOSARC RAAL is a writer and editor originally from Varna, Bulgaria. He is the author of the chapbooks: *[SELF-SELECTIONS]* (Trainwreck Press, 2021), *The Poetry of Carlux Carluxlax* (Reverse Catfish, 2022), and *The Adverse Keys* (Spiral Editions, 2022). A pamphlet, *Dead or Alive* (The Creative Writing Department), was published in 2022. He was tyrant over the poetry and arts journal *NOMATERIALISM* (2020–2022). He is currently composing a book of prose poems entitled *NOTHING*. He has lived in Brooklyn, Greece, Argentina, and Saudi Arabia, and he currently resides with his wife and sons in Los Angeles, CA. Hit him at losarcraal@gmail.com or Instagram @nomaterial_ism.

BLACK SUN LIT is a print and digital literary press that endeavors to introduce, promote, and support both emerging and experienced writers whose work has little representation—or minimal exposure—in a reading world largely governed by commercial publishing.

We propose a renewed aestheticism that values beauty—not communication or identification—as the end of literature. Beauty is for us the experience of the limit, an autonomy beyond that of life itself. We search for it in all forms of extreme expression: whether in minimalism or maximalism, ultramodernism or neotraditionalism, in the experimental or in the archaic, in a desire that exceeds the body or in the longing for boredom. Beauty is the encounter between the saint and the hedonist, the prostitute and the Buddha: a truth that, like staring into the face of Medusa, petrifies the gaze into a contemplation of nothingness. At Black Sun Lit we value beauty that can be discerned in the fragmentary and the sacred, the dysfunctional and the erotic, the derelict and the obsessive.

Subscribe to the BSL mailing list to receive notifications about new print and digital releases, open reading periods, submission guidelines, events, news, and more.

Praise for *No Material*

Does anyone writing now, or even *recently*, make English sound so bristingly and kinetically alive? I don't think so.

—Kirsten (Kai) Ihns, author of *sundaey*

Losarc Raal's poetic notebook is most welcome today when an irreverent, asubjective poetics of modernist-surrealist stripe has been all but silently escorted from the premises of North American poetry, with evil flowers subordinated to a pseudo-left personal, political, or environmentalist moralism. With a vocabulary more alarmingly varied than entire shelves of contemporary verse, this manual against all pieties hammers the conspiracy of marketable somethings. You know nothing of the extreme force of this terrible rupture.

—David Lau, author of *Still Dirty*

In *No Material*, Lorsac Raal. Animatronic graham cracker crust. Lorca Rasal. Show me a rose or leave me alone. Aral Calors. The man who died on television planned to live to be a hundred. Oral Sacral. Viral liverwurst as far as an ass caught in neckwear. Loala Scarr. I wrote at least ten letters. Rascal Rola. Catch me in your inner nest. Lora Scraal. Suddenly impactful mathematical radical. Arc Sallaro. This is not up for debate. Carla Solar. An accidental overdose overdoes it. Cola Larras. Missing masked singer sewing machine swingline staplegun. Sorral Laca. Press the wrong button for the right reason. Carra Llaso. Alright, let's go, you guys. Caral Alors. Alla Carros. Oscar Ralla.

—Garrett Caples, author of *Lovers of Today*